The Traveling Peacocks
Adventures in Texas

Delma & Larry Smith

Dedication

To our dearest friend,
Rosemary Perales —
A creative, dedicated teacher, administrator and a truly loving friend.
You made an immeasurable impact and left a lasting imprint on so many lives.
Thank you for always believing in us, for encouraging every endeavor, and for
walking alongside us with unwavering support.
You gave so much of yourself to others — with a caring heart, strong
leadership, and boundless generosity.
Your spirit lives on in every life you touched, in every lesson you shared, and in
every memory we hold dear.
We miss you deeply and honor you always.
We also dedicate this book to all of the incredible teachers across Texas—
To those who spark imagination with creativity,
Who nurture a love of reading, word by word,
And who pour heart and soul into every lesson.
Your passion for teaching and learning doesn't just fill classrooms—
it lights the way for generations.
This book is for you. Thank you for inspiring your students.

One day the Traveling Peacock decided
he wanted to go on an exciting
adventure to Texas!

"Texas is so big, and I know
I'll see lots of wonderful
things there!" he thought with
a flutter of his feathers.
I want to learn about
Texas.

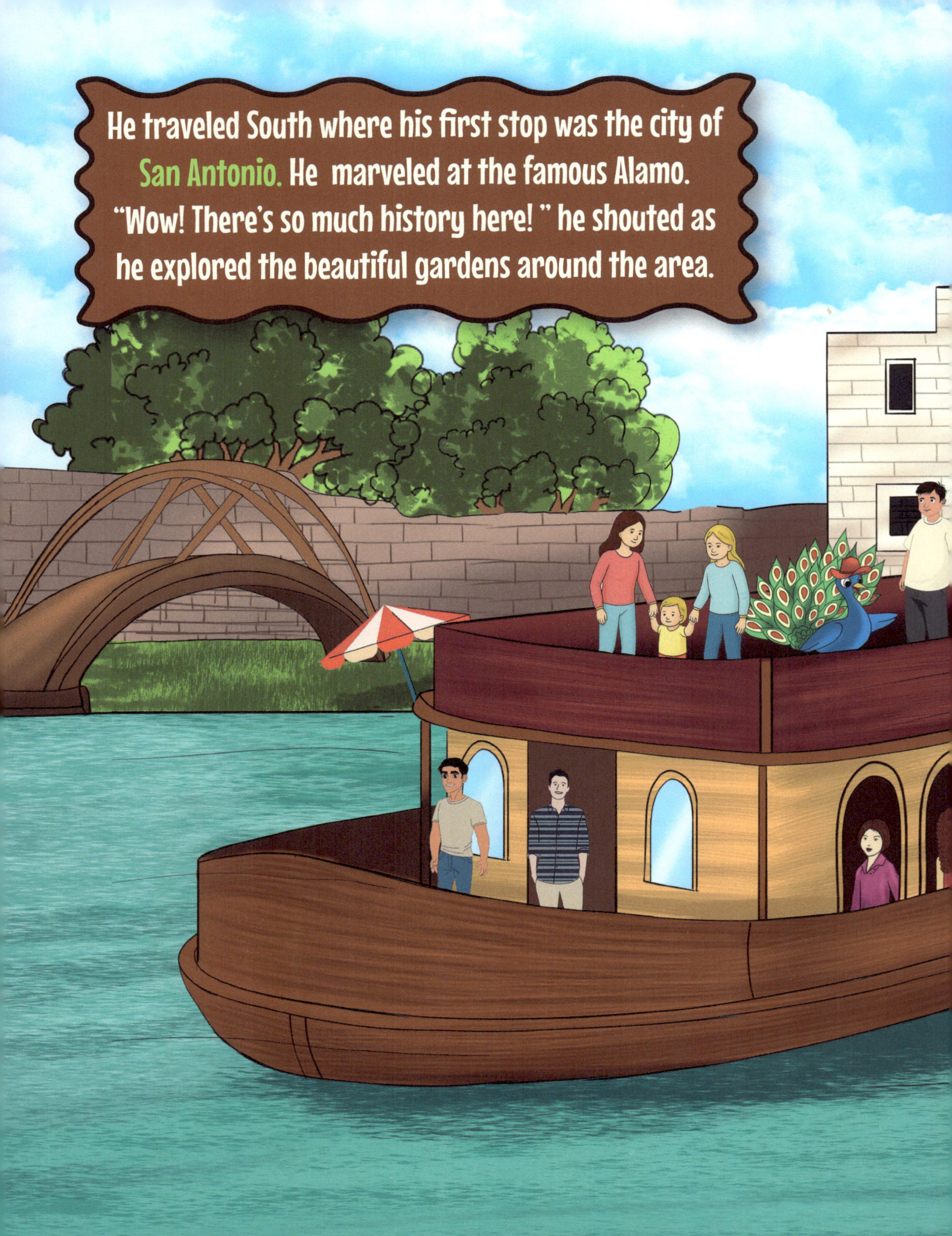

He traveled South where his first stop was the city of San Antonio. He marveled at the famous Alamo. "Wow! There's so much history here!" he shouted as he explored the beautiful gardens around the area.

He even took a stroll along the famous River Walk, where he enjoyed the bright flowers and tasty snacks sold by friendly vendors and beautiful river boats

As he strolled further, he stumbled upon a magnificent shade tree full of nuts. "I love nuts, they are my favorite snack" the peacock mused, curious about their taste.

A friendly squirrel perched high in the branches chimed in, "Those are pecans! They're very tasty." The squirrel graciously shared some, and the peacock learned that the pecan tree is Texas's state tree.

As the peacock listened,
he heard a sweet melody drifting
from the treetops.
"What a lovely song!"
he exclaimed.
"That's the Mockingbird,"
the squirrel said proudly.
"It's the state bird of Texas!"

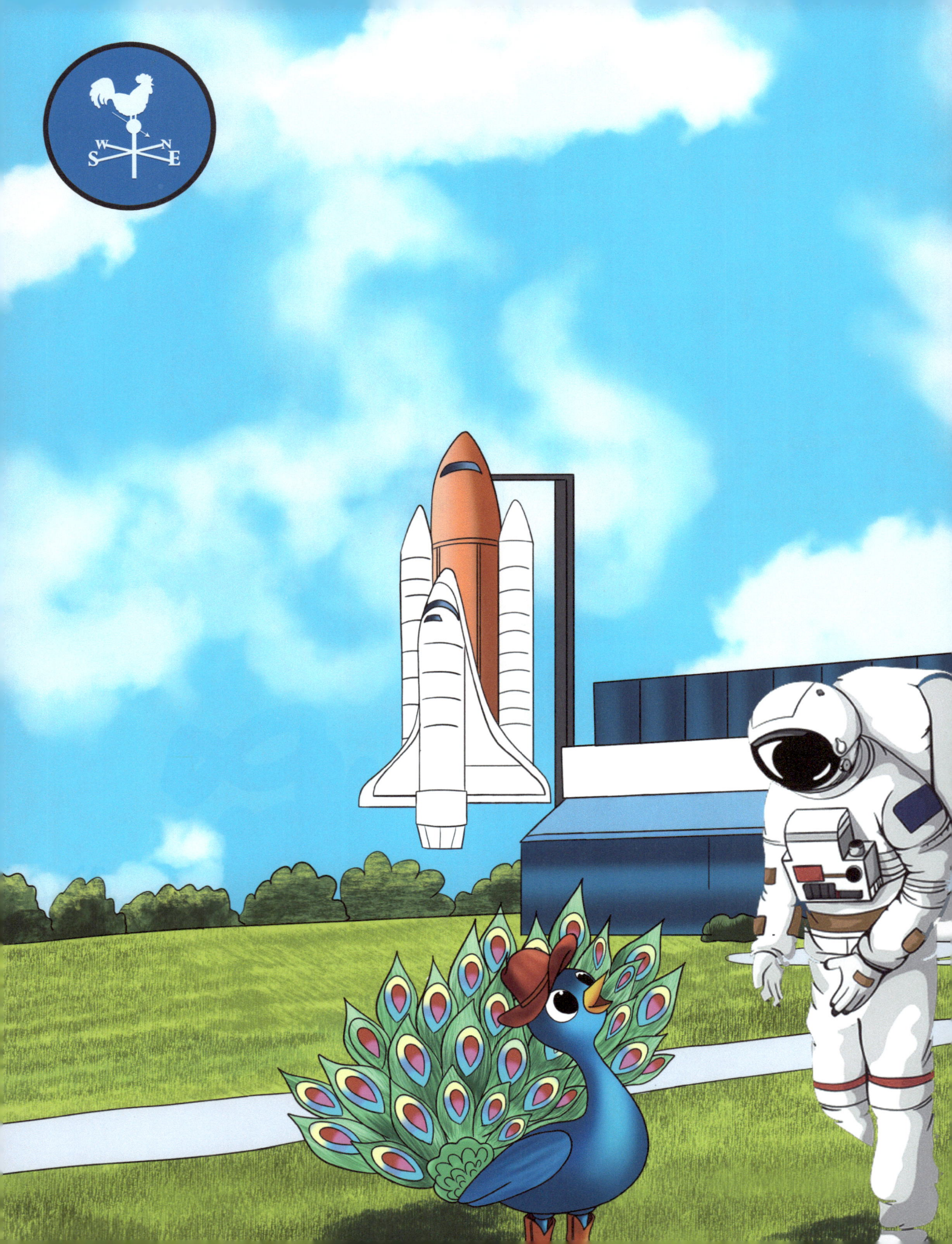

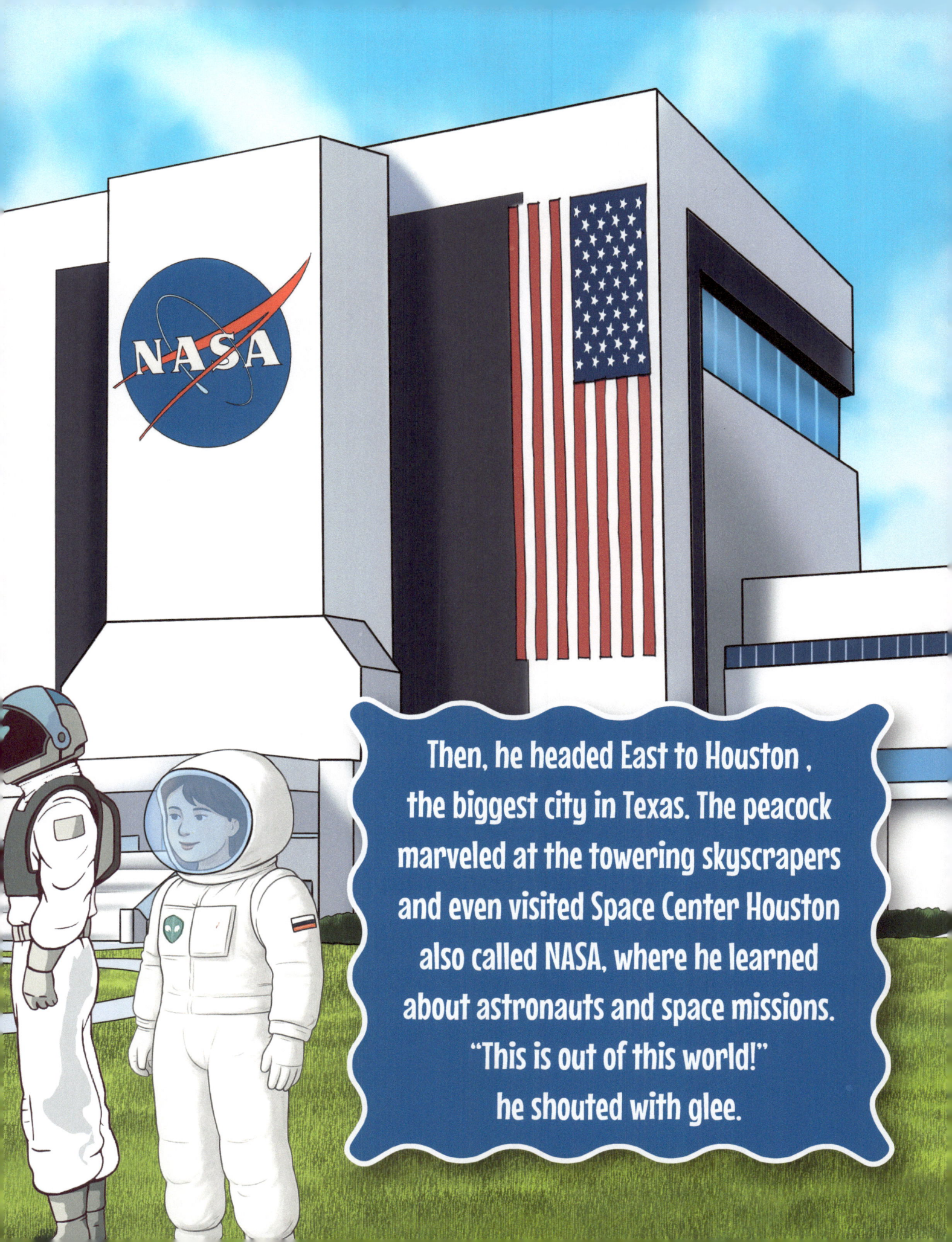

Then, he headed East to Houston , the biggest city in Texas. The peacock marveled at the towering skyscrapers and even visited Space Center Houston also called NASA, where he learned about astronauts and space missions. "This is out of this world!" he shouted with glee.

Along the way he passed a beautiful field of
Bluebonnets.
"What a cute little flower!.
I wonder how it got those little bonnets"

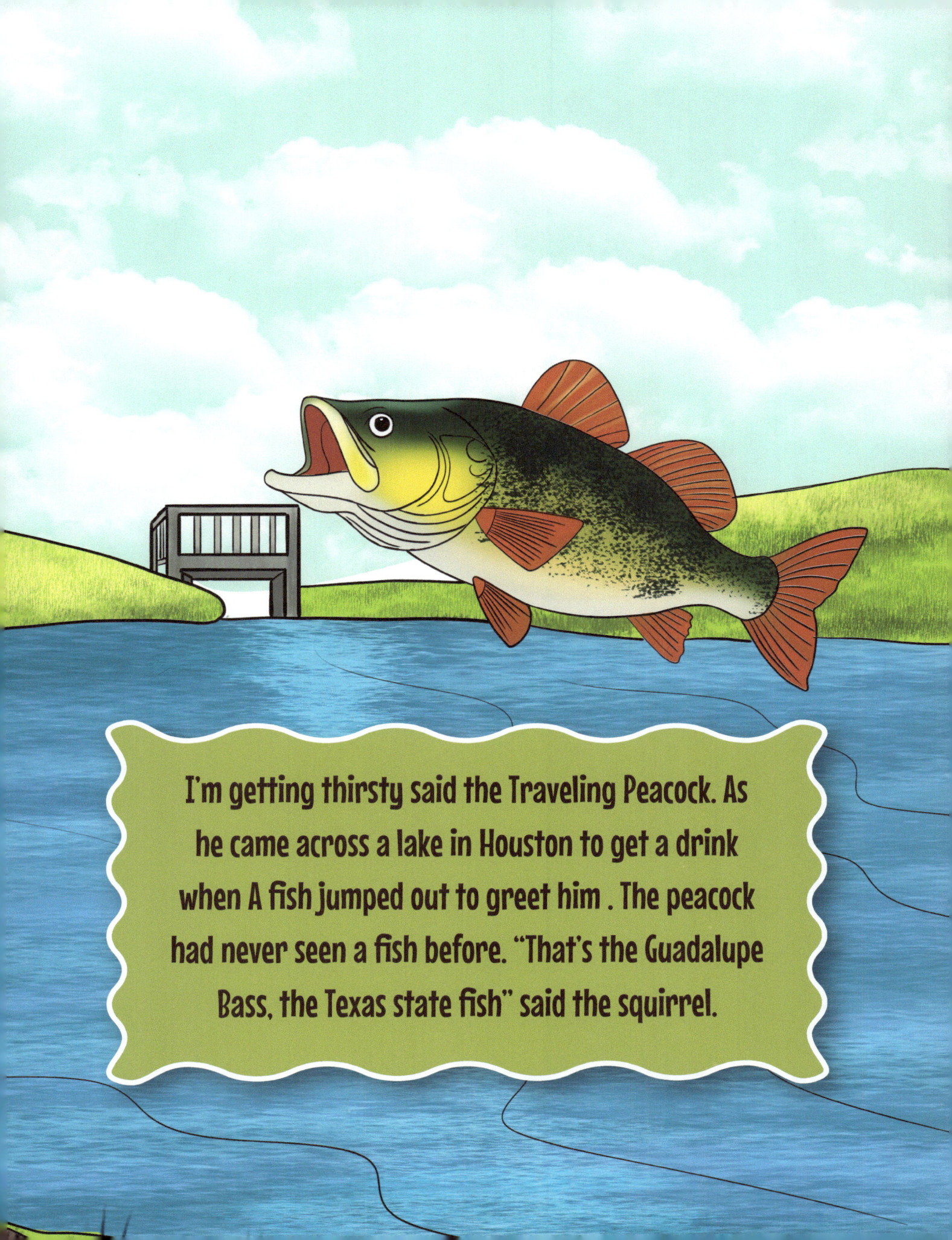

I'm getting thirsty said the Traveling Peacock. As he came across a lake in Houston to get a drink when A fish jumped out to greet him . The peacock had never seen a fish before. "That's the Guadalupe Bass, the Texas state fish" said the squirrel.

6TH FLOOR MUSEUM

He also visited the Sixth Floor Museum, learning more about history while walking through the city's vibrant streets filled with art and culture.

He also had time to visit the Dallas Cowboys football practice field where he high fived some football players. The players gave him a football jersey to take on his trip.

Finally, he made his way West to Amarillo, Texas, where he saw a lively farm filled with all sorts of animals. He saw playful goats, muddy pigs, gentle cows, and tall strong horses, and even a big Texas Longhorn Bull. "What a fun place!" chirped the peacock as he explored.

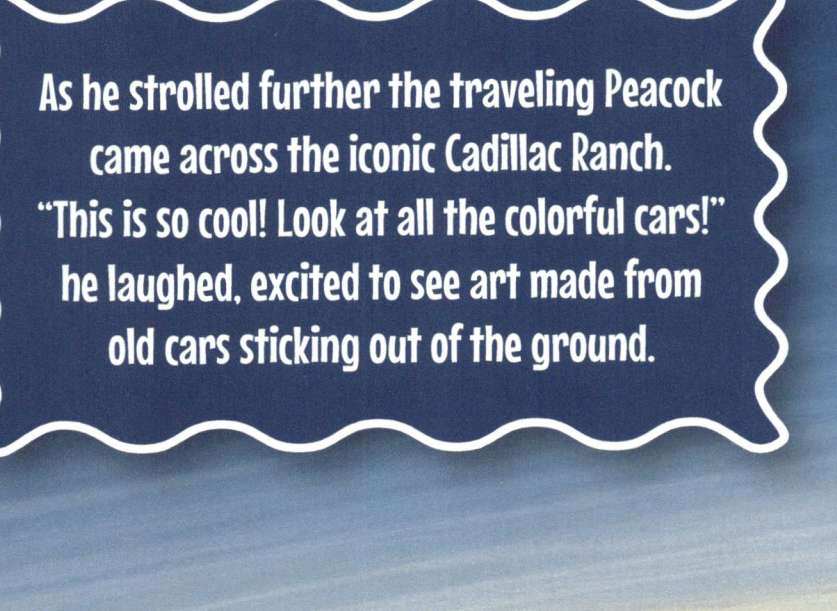

As he strolled further the traveling Peacock came across the iconic Cadillac Ranch. "This is so cool! Look at all the colorful cars!" he laughed, excited to see art made from old cars sticking out of the ground.

As the Peacock got hungry he stopped at Buccees for some famous Texas BBQ, savoring every bite.

The Peacock heard a sound—"Squawk! Squawk!"
Seagulls were calling from far away.
"I wonder where they're going," thought the Peacock.
So, he flew after them, south toward the sea.
Soon, he reached a sunny place called Corpus Christi,
where the sky was blue and the ocean waves sparkled.
He saw boats in a big marina, and people playing on the
beach. It felt like a party by the ocean!

As he walked near the water, he found a pretty statue. It was the Selena Memorial. People were smiling, taking pictures, and listening to music in Spanish. The Peacock swayed to the beat—he liked the rhythm! Selena was a famous Tejano singer and is still very popular for her music.

Then—grrrowl! His tummy started growling. He was hungry.

WHATABURGER

Not far away, he spotted a bright building with orange and white stripes. It was a burger place. The traveling peacock stopped at the very first Whataburger! This Whataburger was first opened in 1950. The traveling Peacock tried a bite of a burger and some fries for the very first time. Yum he fluttered his feathers happily.

Full and happy, the Peacock fluffed his feathers, watched the sunset, and smiled. "Corpus Christi," he thought, "is full of great music, the sound of the ocean And Whataburger!

On his journey, the peacock encountered all sorts of amazing things. He met friendly animals, explored beautiful bluebonnet fields, and learned about the state's symbols and even visited NASA!

The squirrel he had met earlier even joined him for part of the trip. "Can you believe how much fun Texas is?" the peacock exclaimed. "I've learned so many things!"

The squirrel beamed with enthusiasm, sharing even more. "Let me tell you more about the United states flag!

The US flag has 50 stars, each one representing a state in the United States, and 13 stripes for the original colonies. The blue symbolizes bravery, red stands for courage, and white represents liberty."

With a heart full of joy and laughter, the traveling peacock couldn't wait to share his stories when he returned home. He realized that Texas was not just a place, but a wonderful adventure filled with friends, fun, and fantastic discoveries! I loved my adventures in Texas "Where can I go next ?" He wondered.

Texas flag

Texas bluebonnet

Pecan tree

Mockingbird

Guadalupe bass